Faith County

by

Mark Landon Smith

Single copies of plays are sold for reading purposes only. The copying or duplicating of a play, or any part of play, by hand or by any other process, is an infringement of the copyright. Such infringement will be vigorously prosecuted

Baker's Plays
7611 Sunset Blvd.
Los Angeles, CA 90046
bakersplays.com

NOTICE

This book is offered for sale at the price quoted only on the understanding that, if any additional copies of the whole or any part are necessary for its production, such additional copies will be purchased. The attention of all purchasers is directed to the following: this work is fully protected under the copyright laws of the United States of America, the British Commonwealth, including Canada, and all other countries of the Copyright Union. Violations of the Copyright Law are punishable by fine or imprisonment, or both. The copying or duplication of this work or any part of this work, by hand or by any process, is an infringement of the copyright and will be vigorously prosecuted.

This play may not be produced by amateurs or professionals for public or private performance without first submitting application for performing rights. Royalties are due on all performances whether for charity or gain, or whether admission is charged or not. Since performance of this play without the payment of the royalty fee renders anybody participating liable to severe penalties imposed by the law, anybody acting in this play should be sure, before doing so, that the royalty fee has been paid. Professional rights, reading rights, radio broadcasting, television and all mechanical rights, etc. are strictly reserved. Application for performing rights should be made directly to BAKER'S PLAYS.

No one shall commit or authorize any act or omission by which the copyright of, or the right to copyright, this play may be impaired. No one shall make any changes in this play for the purpose of production.

Publication of this play does not imply availability for performance. Both amateurs and professionals considering a production are strongly advised in their own interest to apply to Baker's Plays for written permission before starting rehearsals, advertising, or booking a theatre.

Whenever the play is produced, the author's name must be carried in all publicity, advertising and programs. Also, the following notice must appear on all printed programs, "Produced by special arrangement with Baker's Plays."

Licensing fees for FAITH COUNTY is based on a per performance rate and payable one week in advance of the production.

Please consult the Baker's Plays website at www.bakersplays.com or our current print catalogue for up to date licensing fee information.

Copyright © 1991 by Mark Landon Smith

Made in U.S.A.
All rights reserved.

FAITH COUNTY
ISBN 978-0-87440-073-1
7986-B

Dedication

To Mom, Dad and Valerie

Faith County was first produced March 2nd, 1991 by the Foundation of Arts at The Forum Theatre, Jonesboro, AR with the following cast (in order of appearance):

Mildred Hayworth Carson ....Joanne Burleson
Faye McFaye.....................Cynthia Boyles Moore
Ruthann Barns.............................Dianne Treece
Naomi Farkle .... Gay Jackson
Delbert Fink..................................Randy Story
Luther Carson............................ Tim A. Prater
Violet Farkle ....Jerrie Grady
Gladys Pimbleton .... Trudy Niederbrach
Bubba Bedford .... Chris Chamberlain

Directed by Mark Landon Smith
Production Stage Manager/Costumes: Donald Bagby
Assistant Director: Sarah Richards
Music by David Jackson

Music for FAITH COUNTY is available exclusively through Baker's Plays. Consult our current catalogue for prices and information.

Photo by Amos Bolden

Foundation of Arts, Jonesboro, Arkansas

"Faith County" by Mark Landon Smith

Front row: Dianne Treece
Second row: (L to R) Jerrie Grady, Joanne Burleson, Chris Chamberlain
Third row: (L to R) Gay Jackson, Tim A. Prater, Trudy Niederbrach, Cynthia
    Moore, Randy Story
Director/Written by Mark Landon Smith

CHARACTERS

Mildred Carson	50ish busybody of Mineola who makes everyone else's business her business and doesn't mind telling you exactly what you should do, when you should do it, and who you should do it with.
Faye McFaye	Late 20s. Flirty young checker at the A&P and town tramp. Spends a great deal of time writing bad poetry and may be described as Early White Trash.
Ruthann Barns	40ish. Wife of Revered Ezekiel Barns and local Moral Majority leader.
Naomi Farkle	40ish. Mildred's best friend and worst enemy. Owns the Bee-Luv-Lee Beauty Salon and local ceramics expert.
Delbert Fink	30ish. Local pig farmer and the object of Faye's affections, a feeling which he does not return nor encourage.
Luther Carson	40ish. Mildred's cousin, Naomi's beau and owner of "Luther's Lube and Tune."

Violet Farkle	25-28. Everyone's favorite and the only person in Mineola with any sense.
Gladys Pimbleton	55ish. The eccentric First Lady of Mineola who drinks a bit too much.
Bubba Bedford	Late 20s. Mineola's "village idiot" who works at "Bubba's Gas 'n Go" and always looks like he crawled out from under a car.

SCENE

The Faith County Fairgrounds in Mineola, a town that is located "somewhere in the middle of nowhere in the South"—a place where Beehive hairdos are still the rage and Saturday nights are reserved for the tractor pull in nearby Pickler.

TIME

The present; even though it seems time has stood still in Mineola.

AUTHOR'S NOTE: The characters in this play are real people, not caricatures, who should be played with sincerity.

ACT I

Scene 1

SETTING: We are at the Faith County Fair.

AT RISE: It is mid-morning. There are four lawn chairs, two card tables R ,and an upright piano. Offstage we hear GRUNTS and GROANS as though someone was having great difficulty carrying something. That someone is MILDRED CARSON who staggers onstage, attempting to keep an oversized cardboard box balanced in her arms.

MILDRED. Faye?!? Faye, sugar? (*Pleading and trying to keep her patience.*) C'mon, honey—this box weighs a ton! (*SHE's lost it: her patience, that is.*) Faye!!! You get away from those stockyards this minute and quit teasin' those stupid pigs. We got work to do! Now you get over here before I drop this thing!

FAYE. (*Sweeping in, dressed In "Early White Trash."*) Did you see that little piglet, Mildred? Wasn't that just the cutest thing?

MILDRED. I swear, I feel like I'm on Mutual of Omaha's "Wild Kingdom." Come over here and help me set this thing down! (*Moving toward card table.*) The Eiffel Tower weighs less than this thing does. There ... I guess that'll do.

FAYE. What's in the box?

MILDRED. Just my ticket to local fame and fortune. *This is my art show entry*, and just between you and me I think it's gonna sweep the awards this year!

FAYE. (*Excitedly.*) Can I see it?

MILDRED. (*Setting out paper goods from box.*) No ... not yet. I wanna wait until Naomi gets here before I unveil it so I can gloat. Oh, she'll just die! I've been waitin' for a chance like this for the last five years. Ever since I can remember Naomi has boasted and bragged about her arts and crafts abilities. Well, this year that little Miss is gonna get her comeuppance!

FAYE. Where *is* Naomi?

MILDRED. I don't know and I really don't care. Did you bring the lemonade?

FAYE. Oh! I nearly forgot it! Why I've been so caught up in my poetry that I think I left it in the car. I'll run and go get it. (*FAYE exits with MILDRED calling after her.*)

MILDRED. Well, hurry on up. People'll start gettin' here pretty soon. I swear I don't know why I keep volunteerin' to head up the concessions committee each year. (*To herself.*) People bring some of the barfiest recipes ever concocted.

(*From offstage and gradually getting nearer, we hear a clear VOICE singing "Bringing In the Sheaves." The VOICE belongs to RUTHANN BARNS, the Reverend's wife and local Moral Majority leader. SHE's carrying a small plate.*)

RUTHANN. Why, hello Mildred. I thought I saw you.

MILDRED. I wish they wouldn't put the concessions stand right next to the stockyards. It drives away the customers.

RUTHANN. I brought a plate of Divinity for the bake sale.

MILDRED. How nice. Just set it on the table there somewhere.

RUTHANN. Wasn't that Faye I just saw?

MILDRED. Yep. Can you believe that get-up she's got on?

RUTHANN. It *is* an interestin' ensemble.

MILDRED. More like some kinda costume if you ask me.

RUTHANN. I don't like to be critical ...

MILDRED. Me either, Ruthann.

RUTHANN. ...but it *is* a little revealin'.

MILDRED. A little?!? A piece of string and a band-aid'd cover more skin. And did you see those earrings she had on? Last time I saw hoops that size they had lions jumpin' through 'em.

FAYE. (*Reenters with a large thermal jug. Sing-song.*) Here we are ... (*SHE notices Ruthann.*) Good mornin', Mrs. Barns.

RUTHANN. Good mornin', Faye. How are you?

FAYE. Fine, thank you. Things have just been so crazy this mornin' I don't know where my head is! I left the A&P early to get down here on time and the place was a madhouse! We had twenty-five cents on the Bumble Bee Tuna ... I've never seen such a crowd! And then my car gave out on me, but luckily ...

MILDRED. (*Indicating jug.*) Here, Faye ... I'll take that. (*SHE does so while crossing to table.*) Whew! It feels like it's two hundred fifteen degrees out here!

FAYE. ...but luckily someone happenstanced by and gave me a jump start.

MILDRED. (*Pouring herself a glass of lemonade.*) I'll bet you enjoyed that!

FAYE. (*Ignoring Mildred.*) Are y'all gonna come to my poetry readin' this afternoon?

MILDRED. Poetry?

FAYE. Yeah. It's gonna be sooooo classy. Bubba and Gladys have consented to accent my readin' by playin' a duet for piano and triangle.

MILDRED. You asked Gladys Pimbleton to play the piano for you? Honey, you're nuts!

FAYE. Why? She told me she could play well.

MILDRED. She lied.

RUTHANN. Mildred, she's just beginnin'. (*To Faye.*) She doesn't play *that* bad, Faye.

MILDRED. Yeah, Ruthann's right. She only plays bad when she's sober, so you don't have anything to worry about. She played one Sunday afternoon for the Mineola Society for Cultural Recognition's Charity Garage Sale—sounded like a hamster runnin' on the keys. (*Taking a drink.*) Yeacchhh! Did you put any sugar in this, Faye?

FAYE. Yeah.

RUTHANN. Faye, I didn't even know you wrote poetry.

FAYE. Well actually I didn't either until last week. Oh, Mrs. Barns ... it's just so excitin' when you discover that you have a gift. I mean a *real* gift! Last night I was just lyin' there sleepin' away when I was suddenly hit by a lightnin' bolt of inspiration!

RUTHANN. (*Impressed.*) Oh, my ... are you listenin' to this Mildred?

MILDRED. Faye, you put sugar in this like I'm Joan Collins.

FAYE. So I got up and turned on the light and Just started writin' furiously. I don't know where it all came from ... but then I had to stop.

RUTHANN. Why?

FAYE. Well, Virgil ... no ... Jimmy Jaye; or was it Otis? Hmmm ... anyway, someone told me to turn out the light and get back to bed. That's why I was late this mornin'. That and my car.

MILDRED. Faye, please spare us the gory details of your love life. We're not interested.

RUTHANN. Why were you late dear?

FAYE. Oh, I was drivin' over here in the Pinto when I was suddenly hit by another lightnin' bolt of inspiration. (*To Mildred.*) All the truly great artists get 'em, y'know. So I pulled over and ... (*Noticing someone offstage.*) ... Oh my gosh! Look! Over there by the tractors! It's Delbert! (*Calling offstage.*) Hey! Delbert!

MILDRED. (*Coming in behind her.*) Faye?! Stop makin' a spectacle of yourself! Hey! Delbert! It's me, Mildred! Why don't you come over in a bit and help yourself to a nice, cool, bitter glass of lemonade?

FAYE. (*Seductively.*) He *does* look hot.

DELBERT. (*Offstage.*) I will, Mildred. Sounds good.

FAYE. See you later, Delbert ...

MILDRED. Delbert is Lottie's sweetie, Faye. And don't you forget it!

FAYE. Oh, I don't know about that. You know no man's taken until he says "I do."

NAOMI. (*From offstage in a sing-song.*) Yoo-hoo, Mildred ...

MILDRED. (*Trying to find a place to hide.*) Oh, my stars ... it's Naomi! I've been hidin' from her all day!

NAOMI. (*Entering with a large platter covered with a paper towel, set of rollers under one arm, and a small stack of magazines in her hand.*) Mildred! There you are! Why you've been hidin' from me all day. Hi ya! Ruthann ... Faye.

FAYE. (*Meeting her.*) Hi, Naomi. Did you bring those back issues of the National Know-it-All with you?

NAOMI. (*Handing magazines to her.*) Here you go, sugar.

FAYE. (*Delighted.*) Oh, goody!

NAOMI. I picked them up at the Bee-Luv-Lee when I stopped by to pick up my rollers.

FAYE. I just love to read these! My personal goal in life is to be featured in one of these things.

NAOMI Featured? What for, honey?

FAYE. Oh, I don't know. Just somethin'. Anyone who's featured in here becomes an instant celebrity. I'd be famous. They have this number you can call if you see anythin' weird.

MILDRED. Faye, I cannot believe you waste your time readin' those. They're nothin' but trash!

RUTHANN. I agree with you, Mildred.

FAYE. But Mrs. Barns, they're not trash! They're *very* informative.

MILDRED. Page after page of nothin' but lies ...

NAOMI. (*To Faye.*) I like 'em too, honey. In the April issue there's this fascinatin' article about a woman who lived for three years in her swimmin' pool by teachin' herself to breathe like a fish.

FAYE. Really?

NAOMI Uh-huh. And her family had to sprinkle those little goldfish flakes in the water so she could eat.

MILDRED. Oh, Naomi ... that is about the stupidest thing I've ever heard!

NAOMI. It is not stupid, Mildred.

FAYE. Some of these stories are just real tearjerkers. There was this one about a female contortionist who earned her livin' by wrappin' her legs around her neck then pickin' up a peanut between her upper lip and her nose. Just breaks your heart.

MILDRED. Now there's a talent that'd make a mother proud. I'd be one happy mother if I knew that my daughter could wrap her legs around her neck and pick up a peanut with her nose.

FAYE. Not her nose, Mildred. Between her upper lip *and* her nose.

MILDRED. Whatever. Those things are a complete waste of time. They have nothin' to do with reality. (*Indicating platter in Naomi's hand.*) Is that for the bake sale, Naomi?

NAOMI. Yeah, they're my Naomi Farkle Sparkle Brownies.

FAYE. (*Peeking underneath paper towel.*) Oh, they look yummy! And ... (*Lifting paper towel up.*) ... oh, my! They spell somethin'. N-A-O-M-I ...

MILDRED. Good heavens, Naomi! You and your spellin'! Every time we have any sort of gatherin' you're always arrangin' food or somethin' else into words.

NAOMI. Well I *was* the Faith County Spellin' Champion ... remember?

MILDRED. Haven't you beat that horse to death yet? We all know what a good speller you are.

NAOMI. I won with the word mellifluous. (*Snapping to attention.*) M-E-L-L-I-F-L-U-O-U-S. Mellifluous.

(*RUTHANN and FAYE applaud.*)

MILDRED. Goodnight nurse, Naomi! You were in the third grade!

NAOMI. Good spellin' is like ridin' a bike—it stays with you forever.

FAYE. Oh, Naomi ... I hope you don't mind, but I kinda "borrowed" your spellin' idea for my poetry. I'm endin' all my poems with spellin', sorta like my signature, y'know.

NAOMI. Why Faye ... I'm honored! That's just fine, sugar. (*Beat.*) What's that smell?

MILDRED. The stockyards. Disgustin', isn't it? Just kills your appetite.

NAOMI. (*Sniffing the air.*) No. I know manure when I smell it. It's sweeter.

FAYE. (*Giggling.*) Oh, that must be my new perfume, "Body Language." Do you like it?

MILDRED. Here, Faye—let me smell. (*MILDRED takes a big "whiff" and gags.*)

FAYE. Well ... what do you think?

MILDRED. P-U, Faye—that stuff stinks! I've killed cockroaches with stuff that smells better than that.

FAYE. Delbert certainly does like it. He says it turns him on.

MILDRED. On to what? Hard liquor?

NAOMI. What time is it, somebody?

RUTHANN. (*Glancing at her watch.*) I've got almost eleven.

NAOMI. Good gravy boat Marie! I didn't realize it was so late. C'mon, Mildred. We've got to get over to my booth.

MILDRED. Naomi, I told you already I'm not gonna do it.

NAOMI. Mildred, you promised you would. Now c'mon...

FAYE. You got a booth, Naomi?

NAOMI. Yeah ... it's for the Bee-Luv-Lee. Mildred said she would let me demonstrate my hairstylin' technique on her. C'mon, Mildred. (*NAOMI motions for Mildred to follow her as SHE starts off.*)

MILDRED. Naomi, I told you no! Now it's too hot for me to sit underneath that hair dryer for who knows how long while you flap your gums about your abilities. Let Faye do it.

FAYE. Yeah, I'd love to.

NAOMI. (*To Mildred.*) Faye? (*To Faye.*) I can't do a thing with your hair, honey! Why you'd be better off just to burn it and start all over. (*To Mildred.*) Besides, Mildred promised!

MILDRED. NO!!

NAOMI. (*Turning to Ruthann.*) You talk to her, Ruthann. Isn't there somethin' in the Bible about lyin'?

(*RUTHANN begins to speak, but MILDRED interrupts.*)

MILDRED. Of course there is, Naomi. You should know that. Although I'm not surprised ... not really. You *never* listened in Sunday School.

NAOMI. *You* were the one who never listened Mildred Hayworth Carson!

MILDRED. I did too, listen. Or have you forgotten that it was *me* who won the little blue Bible for bein' the first one to memorize the 23rd Psalm?

NAOMI. The only reason you won is because you taped the words to the inside of your dress! Why with the way that thing was flyin' up and down you would've thought there was a vent in your britches!

MILDRED. That's a lie!

RUTHANN. (*Stepping in.*) Girls!! Mildred, I think since you did promise Naomi you would do it, you should.

FAYE. Yeah, Mildred.

RUTHANN. "Thou shalt not lie" *is* one of the Ten Commandments.

MILDRED. Ruthann ... please don't bark Bible verses at me. It's too hot.

NAOMI. You *did* promise, Mildred.

MILDRED. (*Giving in.*) Oh ... all right, all right, all right! I'll do it!! I swear, anything's better than this persecution!

NAOMI. Oh, goody! I just knew you would. I'm so excited! And I've written a little song to sing while I'm stylin' your hair.

MILDRED. (*Suspiciously.*) A song?

NAOMI. Uh-huh. Sort of like my theme song, y'know. It goes like this: (*To the tune of "Old MacDonald."*)
NAOMI FARKLE IS HER NAME,
E-I-E-I-O
SHE'LL WORK HER MAGIC ON YOUR MANE,
E-I-E-I-O
WITH A LITTLE TEASE HERE,
AND A LITTLE TEASE THERE.

HERE A TEASE,
THERE A TEASE ...
(*Spoken.*) Do you like it?

MILDRED. No.

RUTHANN. I think it's darlin', Naomi. I'm certain it'll get you lots of business.

FAYE. Y'know ... I heard through the grapevine that there's a new shop openin' up in town. Madge's Country Curl.

MILDRED. Oh-oh, Naomi. Competition.

NAOMI. Who? Madge? Oh, I've known her for years. She does pitiful work. Pi-ti-ful! She used to work over at Betty's Beauty Box in Pickler, and her beehives start to fall after only two days! Isn't that just awful? I hate shoddy workmanship in hairdos.

FAYE. What are you gonna do to Mildred's hair?

NAOMI. Oh, I thought I might corn row it and put some beads and stuff in it.

MILDRED. What?

NAOMI. It's the latest. You'll look great.

MILDRED. Naomi, I am not about to let you decorate my hair like a Christmas tree.

NAOMI. Just a few, Mildred. Please?

MILDRED. No! I have no intention of spendin' the rest of the afternoon lookin' like Polynesian royalty. You can play with these spit curls if you like, but that's all.

NAOMI. (*Disappointed.*) Well, all right then. C'mon.

(*MILDRED begins to exit as NAOMI follows.*)

RUTHANN. Naomi, I guess I'd better get back to handin' out my leaflets. May I give some out at your booth?

(*NAOMI stops as MILDRED exits.*)

NAOMI. I suppose so, Ruthann. But please don't sing "Jesus Wants Me for a Sunbeam." It makes people feel uncomfortable and you're a little flat.

RUTHANN. You stayin' here, Faye?

FAYE. Yeah, I'll watch the concessions and finish this article until y'all get back.

RUTHANN. O.k., dear.

MILDRED. (*Storms back on.*) Well c'mon, Naomi! You were the one who was so hot-fired to get out of here in the first place! Mush! Mush!

NAOMI. All right, Mildred! Oh … I'm just so excited!
MILDRED. Oh, shut up.

(MILDRED, NAOMI and RUTHANN exit. FAYE, left alone, takes a napkin and dabs the sweat off her forehead. Suddenly SHE notices someone coming toward her. SHE bolts for a chair pulling another in front for her feet and strikes a "sexy" melodramatic pose while drapping the magazine over her body as DELBERT enters.)

FAYE. Oh, hello … Delbert.
DELBERT. Hey, Faye. Mildred here?
FAYE. (*Hesitates for a moment then assumes a different "Provocative" pose.*) No … she and Naomi have gone over to the Bee-Luv-Lee booth. (*Sexily.*) I'm just sittin' here all alone with beads of sweat pourin' down my lithe and supple figure, readin' a touchin' story about a woman who was raised by a family of beavers and went on to invent press-on toenails. (*Beat.*) Hey … you look like you could use a glass of lemonade.
DELBERT. Yeah. It sure is hot. Is there any ready?
FAYE. (*Lazily while rising to get Delbert's order.*) Uh-huh. (*Pause.*) Why you're just drippin' with sweat. I just *love* a man who isn't afraid to sweat.
DELBERT. That so?
FAYE. Uh-huh. (*Handing glass to him.*) Here you go.

(DELBERT takes drink and "chugs" it.)

FAYE. Delbert?
DELBERT. (*Wiping his mouth with his sleeve.*) Huh?

FAYE. I sure did enjoy that donkey basketball game you took me to last week.

DELBERT. (*Drinking.*) Yeah?

FAYE. And that tractor pull the week before. (*Beat.*) Didn't you have a good time?

DELBERT. Yeah, I guess so. This lemonade needs some sugar.

FAYE. Y'know, Delbert. I've been doin' some thinkin'. (*Pause.*) 'Bout us.

DELBERT. Us?

FAYE. Uh-huh. Y'know ... we've been seein' quite a lot of each other lately.

DELBERT. Faye, we've been to the game, the movie, the pull and eatin' to the Happy Heifer. That's all.

FAYE. And don't forget that mud wrestlin' thing! Why everybody is startin' to talk. My daddy is startin' to ask questions. Well ... wonder, really.

DELBERT. (*Pouring himself another drink.*) What kind of questions?

FAYE. (*Surprised.*) Delbert!!

DELBERT. (*Taking a drink.*) What?

FAYE. About when we're gonna get married!

DELBERT. Married? Now look, Faye. I never said anythin' 'bout gettin' married!

FAYE. You didn't have to. I saw the way you looked at me at the tractor pull.

DELBERT. That wasn't love. That was indigestion.

FAYE. But you've got to marry me! I mean, I've got it all planned out. I thought we could have the ceremony down at the A&P where I work. We could walk down the aisle between the paper products and the potato chips. I was hopin' to get featured in the National Know-It-All for gettin' married in a grocery store! That's always been my dream.

DELBERT. Faye, I ain't ready for marriage.

FAYE. But, Delbert …

DELBERT. (*Interrupting.*) Faye, marriage is the furthest thing from my mind right now. (*Beat.*) Except … *maybe* … to Lottie.

FAYE. But I've been makin' plans for us, Delbert! All my friends think we're gettin' married! My momma has already made one hundred fifty-four weddin' bells out of styrofoam cups and aluminum foil for the reception!

DELBERT. C'mon, Faye … hush up!

FAYE. (*Her voice rising.*) I've already been down to the K-Mart and picked out our pattern! How dare you lead me on like this!

DELBERT. Lead you on? What are you talkin' about?

FAYE. I wouldn't marry you, Delbert Fink, if you were the last person in Faith County! I never want to see you again! (*FAYE begins to exit.*)

DELBERT. Where're you goin'?

FAYE. (*Spinning around.*) To cancel the reservations I made at Duegy's Motor Court for our honeymoon! And that jump start you gave me this mornin' was the worst I've ever had! Goodbye! (*Exits.*)

DELBERT. Faye?!?

(*LUTHER CARSON, Mineola's resident mechanic, enters.*)

LUTHER. Naomi? (*HE notices Delbert.*) Oh, hey Delbert. You seen Naomi?

DELBERT. (*Kicking the ground.*) Nope.

LUTHER. What's wrong, buddy?

DELBERT. That stupid Faye McFaye thought I was gonna marry her! Isn't that just ... stupid?

NAOMI. (*Enters talking to herself.*) Good gravy boat Marie! I swear I need a beeper to keep up with myself. (*To Luther.*) Why hi there Luther, sugar. You seen my rollers?

LUTHER. (*Nervously.*) Uhhh ... no, I haven't.

NAOMI. (*Looking around.*) Where could those suckers be? I'm demonstratin' my hairstylin' technique on Mildred and I finally got her to quit gripin' by givin' her some of those National Know-It All things. And I need to get back and finish her hair before she finishes with 'em. Now where could those things be?

DELBERT. Look, Luther ... I just came over to get a quick glass of lemonade. I gotta get back to my tractors. I'll see ya later.

LUTHER. Bye, Delbert.

(*DELBERT exits.*)

NAOMI. (*To herself.*) Now I know I had those here just a little while ago.

LUTHER. Naomi, honey?

NAOMI. Luther, I don't have time to visit! I've got to find those rollers! Don't just stand there lookin' stupid ... help me look!

(*LUTHER hesitates as NAOMI searches. HE's trying to gather the courage to say something he knows Naomi isn't going to like.*)

LUTHER. Oh ... uh ... butterwings, I've got somethin' I need to talk to you about.

NAOMI. What is it, sugar?

LUTHER. (*Stalling.*) Well ... uh ...

NAOMI. C'mon, Luther ... I've got to get back to my booth.

LUTHER. It's about this arts and crafts competition.

NAOMI. Ohhh ... I'm just so excited 'bout us goin' together. I just know my ceramic bust of Lincoln is gonna win!

LUTHER. Well ... I don't mean to put a damper on your day, but I thought I ought to let you know as soon as possible.

NAOMI. What is it, Luther? Are you sick?

LUTHER. No, nothin' like that. You see, sugar puff, there's this demonstration of this new John Deere four-row fertilizer and I just gotta see it. (*Beat.*) It's the same time as the judgin'.

NAOMI. A fertilizer?

LUTHER. I'm the only one certified to work on that kind of machinery, and ...

NAOMI. (*Interrupting.*) You mean you'd make me go to the craft competition by myself? People snickerin' behind my back, to go see some stupid jumbo fertilizer?

LUTHER. Honeytoes ...

NAOMI. But Luther ... I'm the Chairwoman! I can't go by myself! I need you there for moral support, sugar.

LUTHER. Ahhhh, you don't need me! You've won for the past five years.

NAOMI. But I don't know about this year! Rumor has it that Mildred has entered a ceramic depiction of "The Last Supper" and it's five-to-one she'll win!

LUTHER. I know it leaves you in a spot, sweet lips, but I have to go! They're havin' this seminar on fertilizer repairs and I've *got* to be there!

NAOMI. Don't give me any of your flimsy excuses, Luther!

LUTHER. I'm awfully sorry. I feel just terrible.

NAOMI. (*Fuming.*) That's just fine. Just fine. I'll make it on my own ... somehow.

LUTHER. Naomi ...

NAOMI. You just run along to your little demonstration.

MILDRED. (*Offstage.*) Naomi?

LUTHER. But ...

NAOMI. (*Crying.*) RUN ON, LUTHER!

(*MILDRED enters. Her hair has been moussed, sprayed, blown, curled and permed beyond recognition. It is, in a word, a mess. Fit to be tied and fanning herself with several copies of the supermarket tabloids, MILDRED fires into Naomi.*)

MILDRED. Naomi Louise Farkle! I am about to melt out there! Are you gonna do this ... (*Pointing to hair.*) ... or am I left to my own resources? And if I have to read another article about a two-headed baby who looks like Elvis, I'm gonna puke!

LUTHER. Hi ya, Mildred.

MILDRED. Don't you "hi ya" me, Luther. You lied to me.

LUTHER. I did what?

MILDRED. You lied to me. You told me my car would be ready yesterday and it wasn't. Now when am I gonna be able to get it?

LUTHER. Well, I'm sorry about that, Mildred. But you have this certain size belt that I don't have in stock, and since your car is so big, I ...

MILDRED. (*Interrupting.*) I don't want a biological breakdown of the problem, I just want to know when my car will be ready.

LUTHER. No later than next week.

MILDRED. Next week?!? But I've got to have it by tomorrow!

LUTHER. Well, I've got this loaner car you can borrow until ...

MILDRED. (*Interrupting.*) No thank you! I've seen that loaner car of yours and I wouldn't drive that thing to the scrap heap!

LUTHER. Well, suit yourself then.

(MILDRED watches LUTHER exit.)

MILDRED. How rude! That's the last time I do business at the Lube and Tune for sure! It's all Harry's fault anyway. I don't know why he keeps buyin' me these big, expensive cars. And that thing uses gas like I was drillin' it in the basement. (*SHE notices NAOMI, who, unable to control herself any longer, wails.*) Naomi? What's wrong, honey?

NAOMI. (*Crying.*) Luther!

MILDRED. Ohhhh ... honey, what happened?

NAOMI. He was supposed to take me to the crafts competition.

MILDRED. Well I know.

NAOMI. And now he's not gonna because he's goin' to see this four-row fertilizer demonstration!

MILDRED. A fertilizer?!?

NAOMI. Yeah, and I just don't know what I'm gonna do!

MILDRED. Now don't you worry, sugar. You can find yourself another date.

NAOMI. Who?

MILDRED. Well, how about Bubba Bedford?

NAOMI. Bubba?

MILDRED. Why sure! He's gonna be here later this afternoon to play the triangle for Faye's poetry readin'. You can go with him.

NAOMI. He smells funny.

MILDRED. He does not.

NAOMI. You wouldn't know, Mildred. Your olfactories aren't as sensitive as mine. Oh, what am I gonna do? If I don't find a date I'll never be able to show my face at the Happy Heifer again!

MILDRED. There's bound to be somebody who would take you to the competition.

NAOMI. No … let's face it, Mildred. I've been ruined. I'm a fallen woman.

MILDRED. Or if worse comes to worse you can go with Harry and me.

NAOMI. But I'm the Chairwoman and I gotta get there early.

MILDRED. I'm gonna get there plenty early. I wanna get my ceramic depiction of "The Last Supper" in a prime spot for the judges to see.

NAOMI. Oh, I know what you mean. I've gotta get my Lincoln bust in there, too.

MILDRED. (*Pauses while SHE considers what this means.*) You mean you've entered somethin' this year?

NAOMI. (*Surprised Mildred would think otherwise.*) Well, of course.

MILDRED. (*Containing herself.*) Don't you think that's tacky for the Chairwoman to be enterin' somethin'? Don't you think that'll influence the judges' decision?

NAOMI. Now, Mildred ... you know it's all done by numbers. No one knows whose is whose.

MILDRED. (*Defensively.*) Oh, sure! You're the only one who enters those stink ugly awful gold-leafed presidential busts year after year!

NAOMI. (*Insulted.*) Stink ugly?

MILDRED. You'd think you'd step aside for once in your life and give someone else the glory!

NAOMI. And you think *you'd* win?

MILDRED. If this one-horse town had any sense of international Biblical culture, they would surely vote for "The Last Supper" over one of your Great American Presidents series!

NAOMI. I put a lot of time and effort into my sculptures!

MILDRED. Well I didn't exactly whip mine up over breakfast this mornin'! I have labored months over that masterpiece. (*Indicating box.*) Just look!

NAOMI. (*Glances into box, then looks closer.*) Who's the guy with the chipped beard? And this one's arm's missin'.

MILDRED. (*Looks into box with disgust.*) For the love of ... that Harry is so clumsy! I told him to be careful when he put this in the car this mornin'. The guy with the chipped beard is Judas and the amputee is Peter.

NAOMI. (*Returning to original argument.*) You started doin' ceramics only after I became famous county-wide for my artistic abilities! One little sculpture does not a sculptress make!

MILDRED. Well you're not exactly the Michaelangelo of Faith County! I would hardly put the presidential series up there with David or La Pieta!

VIOLET. (*Offstage.*) Mildred?

MILDRED. Violet? Is that you, sugar? What in tarnation are you doin' up and about? I thought you were supposed to stay off your feet as much as possible!

(*A very pretty and very pregnant VIOLET FARKLE waddles on.*)

VIOLET. Oh ... a little exercise never hurt anyone; especially when you're pregnant. Besides, I couldn't miss the event of the year! Has the judgin' started yet?

MILDRED. It's not 'til this afternoon.

NAOMI. (*Abruptly.*) Excuse me. (*Hurriedly exits.*)

VIOLET. What's wrong with Naomi? She looks upset.

MILDRED. You mean she looks scared to death! She's afraid she's not gonna win the art competition this year. The ole chicken.

VIOLET. What happened to your hair?

MILDRED. Naomi Farkle, the Mineola Beauty Butcher has been hackin' away at my hair for the past half-hour. Watchin' her cut my hair was like watchin' the shower scene in "Psycho."

VIOLET. Oh, I brought some of my appliqued toilet seat covers for the art show. I don't think they should be judged; I just brought them because I thought they might be pretty to look at. (*SHE hands the toilet seat covers to Mildred.*)

MILDRED. (*Taking covers.*) They certainly are. (*Crossing to table.*) We'll just put them over here by my ceramic depiction of "The Last Supper."

VIOLET. Whew! It's hot out here!

MILDRED. (*Helping Violet to chair.*) You wanna glass of lemonade?

VIOLET. Oh, no thank you, Mildred. I'm fine. I think I'll just sit here for a spell and rest.

MILDRED. Well ... tell me, sugar—have you and Bud picked out a name yet?

VIOLET. What? Oh! The baby! Why, as a matter of fact we have. It it's a boy we'll name him Bud Junior, of course ... after his daddy.

MILDRED. And if it's a girl?

VIOLET. Then we'll name her Violet Bud.

MILDRED. (*Dreamily.*) Violet Bud ... Violet Bud Farkle. Why I believe that's the prettiest name I've ever heard. Oh, I hope it's a girl, honey. Girls are so much fun! You can dress 'em up in cute little dresses and buy them sweet dollies and stuff. When's it due?

VIOLET. Any day now and thank goodness! I feel like I was born pregnant!

FAYE. (*Enters.*) She's here, she's here, she's here!! Oh, goody, goody, goody!

NAOMI. (*Enters.*) What're you so excited about, Faye?

FAYE. Bubba and Gladys are here! Luther's helpin' Gladys bring her things in.

NAOMI. I don't care.

MILDRED. Well, my stars, Faye. You're carryin' on like Jackie Onassis just drove up on a tractor.

FAYE. Oh, y'all ... I'm just *sooooo* excited 'bout my poetry readin' this afternoon! I want all of y'all to listen to the poems I've written and give me your true and honest opinion.

VIOLET. We'd be happy to!

FAYE. Y'know, I sent a collection of my poems to Gladys and she loved 'em. Imagine, the recently dumped First Lady of Mineola bein' a fan of *my* poetry!

(Pause.)

MILDRED. What was that you said, Faye?
FAYE. That Gladys was a fan of mine?
NAOMI. No ... before that.
FAYE. That she loved my poems?
VIOLET. No ... after that.
FAYE. Recently dumped?
MILDRED, NAOMI, and VIOLET. THAT'S IT!!!
MILDRED. You know somethin', Faye McFaye ... c'mon, spill it!
FAYE. Oh, shoot! Me and my big mouth!
NAOMI. Faye, you come right over here and sit down right across from me and you just tell us all about it.
FAYE. Oh, I don't know. I gave my word I wouldn't tell.
MILDRED. Your word isn't worth anythin', sweetie. Everyone knows what a big liar you are.
NAOMI. But, that's one of your most endearin' qualities. Tell us!
FAYE. Well ... (*Quickly.*) Mayor Joe Bob told Gladys he was goin' out to pick up a box of Cheese-its, and he never came back.
VIOLET. (*Laughing.*) Oh! How scandalous!
MILDRED. That's it?
FAYE. Well ...
NAOMI. Here it comes ...

FAYE. She then found out through a private detective she hired from Esther Flats that he was havin' a little extra gravy with his potatoes with some hairdresser from Polk City.

MILDRED. Really?

NAOMI. I know exactly who she's talkin' about! I'll bet you anythin' it's Tammy Jane Sprinkle. I always knew she was nothin' but white Christmas trash!

FAYE. But that's not all! (*Looks over her shoulder to make certain no one is overhearing.*) Gladys, soused to the gills, drove down to Polk City and had it out with ...

NAOMI. Tammy Jane Sprinkle. She's an S-L-U-T.

MILDRED. Go on, Faye ... go on!

FAYE. Anyway, Gladys went to where that girl ...

NAOMI. Tammy Jane Sprinkle ...

FAYE. Yeah. She went to where she worked and threatened her with a hot curlin' iron!

VIOLET. (*Laughing.*) No!

NAOMI. I always knew Gladys was psychotic.

MILDRED. Deranged!

NAOMI. No wonder she drinks so much!

MILDRED. I told her one time, "Gladys, you look ...

(*GLADYS, carrying a cake, enters unnoticed by MILDRED but seen by NAOMI.*)

NAOMI. (*Finishing Mildred's sentence.*) ... wonderful!

MILDRED. No, that wasn't it!

NAOMI. (*For Mildred's benefit.*) Gladys, how nice to *see* you!

GLADYS. Greetings and felicitations! Oh, what a glorious day this is! A perfect day for the arts and crafts competition. Al fresco! Here, Miss Farkle, I made my county-famous rum cake for the bake sale.

NAOMI. (*Taking cake from Gladys.*) Thank you, Gladys. (*NAOMI removes cake cover. Suddenly EVERYONE, overcome by the alcohol content of the dessert, reels.*)

GLADYS. I made it from my own secret recipe.

MILDRED. One tablespoon of flour and eight quarts of rum.

GLADYS. Oh, Mrs. Carson ... what an interestin' coiffure. What is it called?

MILDRED. "Sheer Stupidity."

GLADYS. Oh, how I *do* love the out of doors! In my will I have a clause which states that I'm to be buried in the great outdoors. My goodness, but it is swelterin'!

MILDRED. Everybody gets buried outdoors, Gladys.

GLADYS. Oh, no dear. I mean in a specific place.

NAOMI. Where?

GLADYS. Here.

VIOLET. Where?

GLADYS. (*Referring offstage.*) Here, underneath that tree. It has always been one of my favorites. Oh, the humidity is unbearable today!

VIOLET. What a perfectly morbid discussion we're havin'. All this death talk.

FAYE. Oh, Mrs. Pimbleton ...

GLADYS. Gladys, dear.

FAYE. Gladys ... I'm just so excited 'bout your playin' during my poetry readin'.

GLADYS. I am more than happy to do it. After all, I am a great fan of your poetical talents. Oh ... (*Removing a piece of paper from her purse, SHE glances over it then replaces it.*) ... your poetry writin' adds to your already natural "pulchritude."

FAYE. Oh … why thank you. I think.

GLADYS. That is one of my words-of-the-day. I have been improvin' my word power with the help of that fine literary magazine, the *Readers Digest*. "Pulchritude" … it means "beauty."

NAOMI. "Pluchritude" … P-U-L-C-H-R- …

MILDRED. Please, Naomi …

GLADYS. I try to use each word three times a day. My vocabulary is simply "integumentin" the ends of the earth.

(The GIRLS stare at her.)

GLADYS. "Integument" … it means "coverin'" …

NAOMI. "Integument" … I-N-T-E-G …

MILDRED. Naomi, please!

GLADYS. Now, Miss McFaye … where should I set up?

FAYE. Right over here by the piano. I thought I could stand sort of to the side and give my dramatical, poetical readin' whilst you and Bubba play.

NAOMI. Bubba's gonna play?

MILDRED. Of course he is, Naomi. I told you that.

NAOMI. But I didn't know Bubba had any musical talent.

MILDRED. He doesn't.

NAOMI. But Faye just said he played an instrument.

MILDRED. He plays the triangle, Naomi. Bubba is gonna accompany Gladys on his triangle. He's been takin' lessons for months.

NAOMI. Oh!

(BUBBA BEDFORD, owner of "Bubba's Gas 'n Go and Velvet Painting Museum" enters dressed in his station

*uniform and carrying a triangle. He is followed by
LUTHER who is carrying a briefcase.)*

GLADYS. *(To Luther.)* Mr. Carson, how kind of you to
bring in my music. Please set it on the "pulchritudic" piano.
Oh, my dears, I do believe that any moment I will succumb to
the vapors!
NAOMI. *(Sincerely.)* Bubba Bedford ... I didn't know you
had musical abilities! Mildred here just told me you played the
triangle! How impressive!
BUBBA. Thank you, Naomi.
NAOMI. Do you take lessons from the same teacher as
Gladys?
GLADYS. Oh, no dear. I take piano by correspondence.
BUBBA. My imaginary friend taught me how to play the
triangle. He also taught me how to tap dance.
FAYE. Bubba, you come over here and get set-up 'cause
I'm gonna rehearse my segment for y'all. The rest of y'all
have a seat.

*(BUBBA goes to meet GLADYS at the piano who is busy
    shuffling through several sheets of music and setting out
    her metronome. Meanwhile, MILDRED, NAOMI and
    VIOLET are arranging their lawn chairs across from FAYE
    who is off to the side "getting into character.")*

MILDRED. Luther, you come over here and sit by me.
LUTHER. Is that all right with you, Naomi?
NAOMI. Shut up, Luther.

*(LUTHER sits as GLADYS takes her place at the piano with
    BUBBA at her side poised with his triangle.)*

FAYE. O.k., now y'all ... I'm *soooo* nervous! Now y'all, I'm gonna read a couple of poems for y'all to give y'all a sort of a sneak preview of this afternoon. And I want ya'll to tell me what y'all *really* think.

FAYE. (*Crosses to edge of stage and faces her "audience."*) Good afternoon, and thank y'all for comin'. My name is Miss Faye McFaye and I will be readin' selections from my collection of poetry entitled: "Poetry: P-O-E-T-R-Y." Written and performed by me, Faye McFaye. The first one is entitled: "My Love For You."

(*SHE pauses for a moment, clears her throat then signals Bubba and Gladys to begin playing. GLADYS sets her metronome as slow as possible and begins to tickle the ivories totally ignoring the set tempo. SHE plays "Fur Elise" painstakingly slow making several mistakes while BUBBA keeps the metronome tempo with his triangle. As FAYE reads, her recitation becomes more melodramatic.*)

FAYE.
My love for you is like an ocean wave,
Liftin' toward the sandy, large shore,
Preparin' to pounce upon unsuspectin' particles.

The bright, white moonlight
Leaves a trail of light upon the
Deep, dark and wet waters,
Of the big, large, vast sea.

The palms sway to and fro like branches
in the tropical wind.

Birds dip and cry …
Kaaaaaaaaaa!
Kaaaaaaaaaa!
Kaaaaaaaaaa!

This is my love for you.
L-O-V-E
Love.

GLADYS. (*Immediately stops playing and bursts into applause.*) Oh, it's so very movin'!

MILDRED. Yep … it's movin' me straight to the bathroom.

GLADYS. The "integumentation" of the emotions was executed with such precise "pulchritudeness."

FAYE. Did you really like it?

GLADYS. Oh yes, my dear.

FAYE. Really, really, really?

GLADYS. (*Fanning herself.*) Yes, yes, yes!

FAYE. (*Turning to the others.*) What did y'all think?

MILDRED. I thought it stunk.

FAYE. Well, that was my first one and it was a little rough. I hadn't grown into my talent yet. Oh, here's my most recent one. I wrote this about … oh … twenty minutes ago. This one is entitled "Teardrops."

(*SHE signals Gladys to play. GLADYS sets the metronome as fast as it will go yet ignores the tempo. During the course of the reading, GLADYS' playing becomes progressively worse until it DOES sound like "a hamster running on the keys." Meanwhile poor BUBBA is beating his triangle for all its worth.*)

FAYE.
Come back.
Come back to me, my love.
I am nothin' without you.
Like bubbles, blown by a child from a bottle
Shaped like a clown, broken in the wind.

And from the corner of my eye … water.
A small droplet tastin' of salt appears.

Teardrops tricklin' down my cheeks.
T-E-A-R-D-R-O-P-S.
Teardrops.

*(There is a pause. Suddenly GLADYS slumps onto the
    keyboard hitting several keys.)*

MILDRED. *(To Naomi.)* That's the prettiest chord she's
played yet.

*(NAOMI, MILDRED, VIOLET and LUTHER laugh. There is
    a pause.)*

NAOMI. Gladys?

(Pause. GLADYS doesn't react.)

LUTHER. You think she's all right, y'all?
FAYE. Mrs. Pimbleton?
NAOMI. Luther, you go up there and see what's wrong.
She may be sick or somethin'. Go on!

(BUBBA backs away slowly as LUTHER approaches.)

LUTHER. Gladys? (*HE shakes her.*) Gladys? (*HE shakes her again then feels for her pulse.*)
NAOMI. Well?
LUTHER. She's dead.
ALL. Dead?!?
NAOMI. Good gravy boat Marie!
MILDRED. Oh, she can't be dead. She's probably passed out in a drunken stupor. Let me see ... (*MILDRED moves toward Luther and Gladys.*)
NAOMI. Be careful, Mildred.
MILDRED. Gladys? Honey ... wake up. (*SHE shakes her.*)
NAOMI. (*Moving in.*) Is she doin' anythin'?
MILDRED. Nope. There's only one way to find out if she's dead or not. (*SHE leans over Gladys' body and screams into her ear.*) OH, LOOK NAOMI! LOOK WHAT I FOUND. AN UNOPENED BOTTLE OF JACK DANIELS. WHATEVER SHALL WE DO WITH IT?

(ALL wait for a reaction from Gladys. There is none.)

MILDRED. Yep ... she's dead.
FAYE. Eeeewwwwwww!! This is *soooooo* gross!
VIOLET. What are we gonna do?
NAOMI. Shouldn't we call a doctor?
LUTHER. Or the police?
MILDRED. This sure does put a damper on the day, doesn't it?

(GLADYS' body begins to slip from its slumped piano position and falls to the ground. ALL scream and run to get as far away from the body as possible. THEY huddle together. There is a pause as each ONE realizes Gladys is indeed dead and one-by-one THEY break from the group and form a semi-circle around the body until all are looking down at her.)

MILDRED. That sure is an ugly dress she's wearin'.

NAOMI. And her hair looks awful. I wonder who does …

FAYE. … *did* …

NAOMI. … did it for her. If anyone has a brush, I could work on it.

MILDRED. Violet, sugar, I think it's best if Bubba takes you home. I don't think you need to be around all this stress.

VIOLET. Yes, I think you're right, Mildred. Poor Gladys. Where's your wrecker, Bubba?

BUBBA. Down wind of the stockyards.

GLADYS. Eeeeeeeeewwwwwwww!

VIOLET. Mildred? Is there anythin' I can do?

MILDRED. No, honey. You just run on. I'll call you later and let you know what happened.

VIOLET. All right. Bye.

(BUBBA and VIOLET exit.)

MILDRED. Faye? You come with me and help find a phone to call someone. Luther? You and Naomi stay here with the body. C'mon, Faye.

FAYE. (*As THEY exit.*) Who's gonna play for my poetry readin' now? Maybe I should call that number in that magazine? This is pretty weird …

(There is an uncomfortable pause as NAOMI and LUTHER are left alone for the first time.)

LUTHER. Ah ... uh ... hmmmmm. Too bad 'bout Gladys. *(NAOMI doesn't react.)* Ahhh, c'mon Naomi. Y'know it drives me crazy when you won't speak to me.
NAOMI. Good.
LUTHER. Not that it matters now, but ...

(Pause.)

NAOMI. But what?
LUTHER. *(Mumbling.)* I'm not goin' to the fertilizer demonstration.
NAOMI. What?
LUTHER. I'm not goin' to the fertilizer demonstration! I decided that I'd rather go to the craft competition with you instead. So ...
NAOMI. Luther, in light of recent developments, I sincerely doubt any of us will be goin' to the craft competition. It's too late now, anyway.
LUTHER. But I decided that long before Gladys died.

(Pause.)

NAOMI. You did?
LUTHER. Sure, schnookie lumps.
NAOMI. You mean you'd do that for little ole me?
LUTHER. Of course I would, sweet cakes. Why you know you're the spark in my carburetor.

NAOMI. (*Crying.*) Oh, sugar plum ... that's about the sweetest thing I ever did hear!

(*Pause.*)

LUTHER. Naomi ...
NAOMI. Yeah?
LUTHER. I know this may not be the best time or the best place, but ...
NAOMI. But what?
LUTHER. I was wonderin' if ... (*Disgusted.*) Ah, I can't do it!
NAOMI. Sure you can sweetie. There's no one here but you, me ... (*Looking down at body.*) ... and Gladys. Now what is it?

(*Pause.*)

LUTHER. (*Mumbling.*) Why don't you ... y'know—park your car in my garage.
NAOMI. What?
LUTHER. Permanently.
NAOMI. (*Pause. SHE is dumbfounded.*) Luther ... are you ... are you askin' me to marry up with you?
LUTHER. Well ... yeah ... I guess so.
NAOMI. Oh, sugar pop ... yes! Yes! Yes! (*NAOMI rushes toward Luther tripping over Gladys' body which is lying between them.*) Oh!
LUTHER. Oh, love lips ... are you all right?
NAOMI. Yeah ... I'm fine. Sorry, Gladys. (*To Luther.*) Oh, sweet potato ... I'm so happy! (*SHE throws herself into his arms.*)

(MILDRED and FAYE enter.)

NAOMI. (*Euphoric.*) Oh, Mildred! Faye! You won't believe what just happened!
MILDRED. Now Naomi, calm down! You're all flushed!
NAOMI. Oh, it's the excitement, I guess.
FAYE. (*Noticing body.*) Whose footprints are these on Glady's legs?
NAOMI. Mildred, Faye ... I'm gettin' married! Next month!
MILDRED and FAYE. What?
NAOMI. That's right ... I'm gonna be a blushin' Bride. Oh, I'm so happy!

(MILDRED, FAYE and NAOMI all embrace forming a small circle. Ad-lib "happy noises" while jumping up and down.)

MILDRED. (*Breaking from circle and running toward Luther. SHE, too, trips over Gladys.*) Oh!
FAYE. Eeeewwwwww, Mildred. You touched her!
MILDRED. My stars ... congratulations, Luther, honey.
LUTHER. Thank you, Mildred.
MILDRED. (*To Naomi.*) Have y'all decided where you're gonna have the ceremony?
NAOMI. Oh, I dunno. We may just elope-like off.
MILDRED. Elope?!? Why you can't possibly elope! Don't be silly, Naomi. You've got to have a big church weddin' with flowers and bunches of people. Let's see ... we'll have Ezekiel officiate, of course, and naturally I'll sing.
FAYE. Mildred, it *is* Naomi's weddin'. Don't you think that she should plan it herself?

MILDRED. But she'll need help, won't she? Why there are showers to plan and parties to attend! Oh ... it'll be so excitin'! Oh, and Naomi, unless you've already decided to register with someone else, "Uncle Bob's Bargain Barn" has some lovely chinette patterns.

NAOMI. I don't want any showers or parties. And I've got dishes, Mildred.

MILDRED. That's right, Naomi. Take the fun out of everythin'. Of course you want parties! Just think of all the loot you can cash in on.

NAOMI. Mildred, Luther and I just want a simple weddin'. We'll probably just have a simple ceremony with just a few of our dearest friends.

FAYE. What about the reception?

MILDRED. Faye's right.

NAOMI. I don't want anything fancy. Just some cold cuts will be fine.

MILDRED. Well, that's real romantic, Naomi. Why don't you have the guests brings their own condiments, too? What are you gonna use for the weddin' cake? A couple of Little Debbie snack cakes?

FAYE. Don't you worry about it, Naomi. *I'll* take care of the Bridal buffet! (*Prounounced "buff-it."*)

NAOMI. (*Excitedly.*) Hey! I know of the perfect place for us to get married, angel toes.

LUTHER. Where?

NAOMI. Right here!!

MILDRED. Here?!?

NAOMI. Sure. Right where Luther proposed to me. Isn't that just too romantic.

LUTHER. Hey ... that is a good idea at that!

MILDRED. You seem to have forgotten somethin', Naomi. Or should I say someone.

NAOMI. Who?

MILDRED. Gladys.

NAOMI. She's dead.

MILDRED. Exactly. Naomi, you're gonna be gettin' married on the exact spot where Gladys bought the farm!

FAYE. Eeeewwwwww! I think that's sick, Naomi.

MILDRED. And that's not all. Did you forget what Gladys told us about where she wants to be buried? Under that tree. Naomi, you're gonna be gettin' married in a cemetery!

FAYE. Eeeewwwwww! Grody! I'm sorry, Naomi ... I won't be able to come.

NAOMI. But Faye, you've gotta! What about my reception? And I was hopin' you'd read some of your poetry.

FAYE. I'm in, Mildred.

MILDRED. Well I think you're all just demented! Just a bunch of sickos!

NAOMI. And I'm hopin' you'll sing, Mildred.

MILDRED. Love to.

(Distant SIRENS drawing nearer.
Slowly ALL turn toward the direction of the sirens as their
eyes fall on the unclaimed rum cake.)

MILDRED. Who gets dibs on the rum cake? (*Quickly.*) One, two, three ... go!

(Four HANDS shoot into the air.)

BLACKOUT
End of Act I

ACT II

Scene 1

SETTING: Same place one month later. Not much has changed. To the side stands a tombstone, decorated with tissue bells and paper doves, on which "Pimbleton" has been etched. Toward the back, facing the audience, are the two card tables arranged side by side with "wedding foods" arranged on top. To the right is a free standing portable toilet, next to which is a small vanity, on top of which rests a mirror, brush, curlers, make-up, etc.—this is Naomi's dressing area. Also on the ground is a small tape player.

AT RISE: As the act opens we find MILDRED pounding furiously on the Porta Potty door.

MILDRED. (*Knocking.*) Naomi? (*MILDRED waits for a moment for a response then pounds with twice the determination.*) Naomi Farkle! You come out of there right now! You're bein' ridiculous.

(RUTHANN enters.)

NAOMI. (*From inside Porta Potty.*) I'm not comin' out Mildred Carson! I just can't go through with it!
RUTHANN. What's wrong, Mildred?

47

MILDRED. Oh, Ruthann! Am I ever glad to see you! Get over here and see if you can talk some sense into Naomi. She's gettin' cold feet and locked herself in the Porta Potty refusin' to come out.

RUTHANN. Oh, dear! This is awful! (*Raps gently on door.*) Naomi? Naomi, honey?

NAOMI. Who is it?

RUTHANN. It's Ruthann, dear.

NAOMI. Hi ya, Ruthann. How are you?

MILDRED. For the love of … Naomi you come out of there right now! You've got a weddin' to attend!

RUTHANN. Naomi, honey? What's wrong, sugar? Are you all right?

NAOMI. I'm fine. I just don't want to get married … that's all.

MILDRED. (*Impatiently.*) Naomi …

RUTHANN. Now, Naomi … today is your weddin' day. The happiest day of your life. You give yourself to Luther and he gives himself to you, and you become one for life. Isn't that beautiful?

MILDRED. Lovely. C'mon, Naomi!!

RUTHANN. Naomi … don't you love Luther?

NAOMI. Of course I do.

RUTHANN. And doesn't he love you?

NAOMI. Yeah … I guess he does.

MILDRED. All right then, that settles it. You love him and he loves you and everything is peachy. Now come out of there this instant! You've got my bridesmaid dress in there with you and I need it!

NAOMI. Oh … all right. (*Door to Porta Potty opens as NAOMI, dressed in slip, kimono, and large house slippers, comes out.*)

MILDRED. (*Reaching past Naomi for dress.*) Thank the heavens! You wouldn't want your Matron of Honor walkin' down that aisle naked, would you?

NAOMI. (*Visualizing.*) I sure wouldn't.

RUTHANN. Naomi, I'm so sorry Ezekiel wasn't available to officiate. We didn't expect that revival in Pig Holler to last this long.

NAOMI. Oh, that's all right, Ruthann. I understand. Lucky for us Bubba wrote off for that Divinty degree he got out of the back of that Popular Mechanics Magazine.

MILDRED. I don't know what this world's comin' to when Bubba Bedford, the village idiot, can get a Divinity degree.

RUTHANN. I don't know, Mildred. I think Parson Bedford has a nice ring to it.

MILDRED. I sure hope my voice warms up all right. I'm just scared to death of crackin' during' "Ah, Sweet Mystery." Those high notes are just murder!

NAOMI. I suppose I should apologize. I don't know what came over me. For a moment there I wanted nothin' more than to be a million miles away from here. Oh, Mildred ... did you ever find anyone to play "The Weddin' March" for me?

MILDRED. Nope, piano players are pretty scarce around here since Gladys died.

ALL. (*With bowed heads.*) God rest her soul.

MILDRED. But I got Harry's tape player and Bubba's got a tape of some weddin' music he's supposed to bring, so I guess that'll have to do.

LUTHER. (*Dressed slovenly in a tux, enters.*) Where's my little bride-to-be?

NAOMI. It's Luther! He's not supposed to see me!!

MILDRED. Run for the Porta Potty, Naomi!!

(NAOMI jumps up and lunges for the toilet slamming the door behind her.)

MILDRED. Luther Carson, what do you mean bargin' over here unannounced like this?!? Don't you know it's bad luck for the groom to see the bride before the ceremony?

LUTHER. Awwww ... I don't believe in that sort of thing.

MILDRED. What do you want anyway?

LUTHER. Oh, I just came over here to give Naomi somethin' to wear.

MILDRED. To wear?!? What on earth could you have that she would possibly want to wear?

LUTHER. Well ... y'know that old tradition? Somethin' old, somethin' new ...

MILDRED. *(Interrupting.)* ... somethin' borrowed, somethin' blue ... yes, Luther, I do know it. So?

LUTHER. Naomi told me yesterday that she had everythin' but the somethin' borrowed, so I thought I'd give her somethin'.

RUTHANN. Isn't that romantic.

MILDRED. Well, what is it?

LUTHER. It's this commemorative lapel pin I won last year at the State Mechanics Convention. *(LUTHER models pin to Mildred.)*

RUTHANN. Isn't that nice, Mildred?

MILDRED. It sure is pretty, Luther, but I don't think Naomi would want to wear a gold-plated carburetor on her weddin' dress.

NAOMI. *(From inside Porta Potty.)* Yes I would!

MILDRED. Naomi you be quiet! You aren't supposed to talk to Luther!

LUTHER. Hi ya, sweetpea.

NAOMI. Hi, Luther.

MILDRED. Don't answer him, Naomi, or you'll be doomed. Now be quiet!!

NAOMI. I'm sorry.

RUTHANN. I think that's terribly nice of you, Luther. I'll be sure and give it to Naomi.

LUTHER. Thank you, Ruthann.

MILDRED. Luther, how did you get over here anyway?

LUTHER. Bubba brought me and Delbert over in his wrecker.

MILDRED. Oh. Did y'all happen to pass Faye?

LUTHER. Nope.

MILDRED. I swear that girl would be late to her own weddin'. Well, when and *if* she gets here y'all send her on over, will ya?

LUTHER. Sure thing.

MILDRED. Now you go back over there and tell Bubba we'll need some more time.

LUTHER. Some *more* time? How much more time?

MILDRED. Do I look like I have a sundial on my forehead? I don't know how much more time ... just some.

LUTHER. What do you need some more time for?

MILDRED. We've got to finish gettin' Naomi beautiful for you, and believe me that's takin' some doin'.

LUTHER. What are we gonna do until you're ready?

MILDRED. Luther, would you quit barkin' questions at me! What do I care what you do? Sit in the car and listen to the radio. When we're about ready I'll send you a signal.

LUTHER. A signal?

MILDRED. Yes, Luther, a signal.

LUTHER. Somethin' like a secret signal?

MILDRED. (*Impatiently.*) Yes, Luther ... somethin' real subtle like shootin' off flares and yellin' "Luther, get your butt over here!"

LUTHER. Oh, all right, but don't you think that'll offend Mrs. Barns?

MILDRED. Luther, get out of here.

LUTHER. Well hurry up. It's awful hot.

MILDRED. Beauty is a thing that can't be rushed. Especially on Naomi. Now scat.

LUTHER. See y'a later. (*To Naomi through Porta Potty door.*) Bye, dumplin'!

NAOMI, Bye, Luther.

(*LUTHER exits.*)

MILDRED. Naomi, shut up!

(*Pause.*)

NAOMI. Is he gone yet?

RUTHANN. Yes, dear. You can come out now.

(*Porta Potty door opens as NAOMI exits.*)

MILDRED. (*Indicating vanity.*) Now you come on over here and sit down, Naomi, and let Ruthann put this baby's breath in your hair.

(*NAOMI crosses to vanity and sits while MILDRED hands RUTHANN a plastic sack which contains enough baby's breath for twenty brides.*)

MILDRED. And I'm gonna go over to the bathhouse and put on my dress. Oh, I just can't wait to see it! (*MILDRED starts to exit.*)

NAOMI. Mildred, why don't you just change in the Porta Potty? I'm not usin' it.

MILDRED. And leave myself exposed to the hoodlums waitin' to pounce upon beautiful young women? *No thank you.*

NAOMI. (*As MILDRED exits.*) You'd be all right.

(*FAYE, carrying two small cans, enters wearing her bridesmaid's dress which has been customized as only Faye could do it. Meanwhile RUTHANN begins to arrange the baby's breath in Naomi's hair.*)

FAYE. (*Singing.*)
GOIN' TO THE CHAPEL AND YOU'RE (*Beat.*)
GONNA GET MARRIED ...

RUTHANN. Faye! Well, it's about time! Where on earth have you been?

FAYE. I'm sorry I'm late, girls. I had to stop down at the A&P and pick up a couple more cans of nuts for the buffet, and then I started readin' the latest issue of The National Know-It-All and got enthralled in this story about a man whose wife turned into a werewolf every time she heard "Da Do Run Run." Isn't that bizarre?

NAOMI. What'd they do?

FAYE. They had to burn all copies of The Shirelles' albums. Oh, Naomi where'd you want the nuts?

NAOMI. Well, Faye ... I don't know. I'm not in charge of the buffet ... you are.

FAYE. (*Crosses to table and sets cans down.*) Oh, Naomi … what a happy day this must be for you. I'm sure you're thrilled to *finally* be gettin' married. (*Through her tears.*) And you realize, don't you, that now that you're gettin' hitched that I'm the only single girl left in Faith County.

NAOMI. Now don't you worry, sugar. Why you'll get yourself a feller.

FAYE. You think so?

NAOMI. Why sure. Why you'd be surprised what men will settle for once they get desperate, so you just don't need to worry.

FAYE. (*Brightening up.*) Well, in honor of this special day, I have a surprise for you.

NAOMI. A surprise?

FAYE. Un-huh. I've written a very special poem to be read durin' the ceremony.

NAOMI. A poem? (*Insincerely.*) Oh, Faye … how excitin'! I just hope we have enough time.

FAYE. What do you mean?

NAOMI. Well, Mildred is gonna sing "Oh, Sweet Mystery" and Bubba's doin' the music and you know Luther and I have written our own vows. And I've gotta take the weddin' pictures with my Instamatic. I'm quite a shutterbug, y'know.

VIOLET. (*Stumbles in on the edge of giving birth.*) Hi, girls.

RUTHANN. Violet, honey … are you all right?

VIOLET. (*Indicating her stomach.*) Is the Hindenberg cleared to land?

FAYE. You look awful.

VIOLET. Well, of course I look awful, Faye. I've been luggin' this kid around with me for three years and I have this fear that it's not gonna be born before its sixteenth birthday. I haven't slept in nights.

NAOMI. Yeah, I know what you mean. I haven't been sleepin' well myself lately.

RUTHANN. Nervous about the weddin', dear?

NAOMI. Yeah, I guess so. I keep havin' this reoccuring nightmare that I'm marryin' Tennessee Ernie Ford and my mother-in-law is Minnie Pearl.

FAYE. I bet you're dreamin' that because you're going' to Nashville for your honeymoon. I'm into dream analysis, y'know ... it's fascinatin'.

VIOLET. Where's Mildred?

NAOMI. She's changin'.

MILDRED. (*Enters in her dress which has been appliqued profusely with Naomi's flower, the daisy.*) Naomi, these are the ugliest dresses ever created!

RUTHANN. Oh, Mildred ... you look beautiful!

MILDRED. Good heavens, Naomi ... I look like a Munchkin!

FAYE. Hi, Mildred.

MILDRED. And you look like Tinkerbell. (*To Naomi.*) I was scared to death walkin' over here from the bathhouse for fear some hive of bees would mark me for their dinner. Who did these for you anyway?

NAOMI. Anabell Wades designed them and I think they're pretty. (*Defensively.*) Pretty, pretty, pretty!

MILDRED. Anabell Wades is blind as a bat and dumb as dirt!

RUTHANN. Now, Mildred ... she isn't dumb. She's just easily confused.

MILDRED. That's puttin' it politely. You remember when she had her baby and her husband bought her a puppy for a welcome home present?

FAYE. (*Remembering.*) Oh, yeah ...

RUTHANN. She named the baby Spot and bought the puppy a car seat!

VIOLET. Isn't that just awful? How could anyone confuse a baby with a dog?

RUTHANN. Well ... it wasn't a particularly attractive child.

NAOMI. Well, I don't care what you think, Mildred. It's my weddin' and I think the dresses are pretty. Pretty, pretty, pretty!

MILDRED. They're ugly, Naomi and I feel like an idiot. (*Noticing the buffet.*) Oh, my stars, Faye!

FAYE. What?

MILDRED. These nuts you brought. These aren't nuts!

FAYE. They are, too!

MILDRED. They are not! These are garbonzo beans! And nobody in their right mind puts the pickle loaf beside the tea mints!

VIOLET. (*Feeling her stomach.*) Oh ... my goodness!

RUTHANN. Violet, are you all right?

VIOLET. Yeah ... I'm o.k. ... Violet Bud or Bud Junior's just kickin', that's all.

NAOMI. (*Glancing at her watch.*) Oh, goodness. I'd better be gettin' on my weddin' dress. We gotta be done by six thirty.

RUTHANN. What for?

NAOMI. "Current Affair."

MILDRED. I guess you're about as ready as you're ever gonna be, Naomi. Ruthann, Faye ... y'all help Naomi into her dress and get lined up. I'll call the boys over.

(NAOMI, RUTHANN and FAYE cross over to Porta Potty where THEY pour NAOMI into her wedding dress. MILDRED goes to the edge of the stage and calls:)

MILDRED. Luther? *(Pause. Louder.)* Luther? *(Pause. Screaming.)* LUTHER, GET YOUR BUTT OVER HERE! *(To herself.)* Good heavens.

(LUTHER, BUBBA, dressed in a priest's outfit, and DELBERT enter.)

LUTHER. *(To Mildred.)* Are we about ready?
MILDRED. Just about. Y'all just wait over there and I'll give you the signal.
LUTHER. What kind of signal?
MILDRED. LUTHER, JUST GO OVER THERE AND WAIT!
LUTHER. O.k.

(LUTHER goes back to where the rest of the MEN are standing as MILDRED turns back to where RUTHANN, NAOMI and FAYE are getting ready.)

LUTHER. *(To the men.)* Oooowee ... am I ever nervous! Is my tie straight?
DELBERT. Yeah, but your fly's open.

(LUTHER zips up his pants.)

BUBBA. Now, Luther ... you remember what to say? According to my Parson's manual ... (*Which HE opens up.*) You're supposed to say ...

LUTHER. (*Concentrating.*) "I do?"

BUBBA. Yeah ...

MILDRED. (*Crossing back to Bubba with tape player in hand.*) Bubba? You got that music tape you were supposed to bring?

BUBBA. (*Handing tape to Mildred.*) Here you go, Mildred. It's on side A.

MILDRED. Well, don't give it to me, Bubba. You're in charge of the music. When you're ready to play it just put it in this tape player thing. (*Handing player to Bubba.*) And make sure the volume's up. Here's my "Ah, Sweet Mystery" tape. (*MILDRED hands cassette tape to Bubba.*)

BUBBA. O.k.

MILDRED. All right then ... I guess we're about ready then. (*Turning back to Naomi.*) You ready, Naomi?

NAOMI. I gotta get my veil on. Just a second. (*NAOMI enters the Porta Potty closing the door behind her.*)

LUTHER. Oh, I think I'm gonna be sick.

(*MILDRED crosses back to Porta Potty.*)

NAOMI. O.k., I'm ready.

LUTHER. Oh, I *know* I'm gonna be sick.

MILDRED. (*Addressing Faye, Ruthann and Violet, who's still in her lawn chair.*) C'mon girls, we're about to start. Get lined up.

(The GIRLS line up behind RUTHANN bunched in front of the Porta Potty.)

MILDRED. *(As VIOLET struggles to get up.)* Well, c'mon, Violet. You're holding up the ceremony!

(VIOLET struggles up and taking her chair with her, falls in line behind FAYE immediately setting her chair down and sitting in it. The bridesmaids should be in the following order: RUTHANN, FAYE, VIOLET and MILDRED in front of the Potty.)

VIOLET. I don't feel so hot.
MILDRED. Lucky you. I'm about to burn up. *(To Bubba.)* Bubba, you boys get set up and put the tape in that tape player thing.

(BUBBA places LUTHER and DELBERT and then turns to the tape player and inserts tape, turns up the volume and presses the start button. Suddenly Hawaiian wedding music explodes on the speakers. EVERYONE is jolted.)

MILDRED. For the love of ... turn it down, will ya?

(BUBBA turns down the volume.)

MILDRED. *(Referring to music.)* What is that anyway?
BUBBA. *(Loudly.)* Hawaiian weddin' music.
MILDRED. Good night nurse.
NAOMI. I like it.

(FAYE begins to cry.)

RUTHANN. Faye, honey … are you all right?

FAYE. (*Crying.*) Yeah, I'm fine. It's just that a weddin' always makes me cry. (*To Naomi through the Porta Potty.*) Oh, Naomi … I think you and Luther writin' your own vows is so romantic. Have you had a chance to look at his nuptials?

NAOMI. Certainly *NOT*, Faye! Not before our weddin' night…

MILDRED. Naomi, what on earth are you still doin' in the toilet? You'd think you could wait until after the ceremony!

NAOMI. I'm waitin' to make my grand entrance.

FAYE. Now when do I read my poem?

MILDRED. A poem? Don't tell me you're gonna waste our time by readin' some of your poetry?

FAYE. Naomi said I could. Didn't you, Naomi?

NAOMI. Yeah, I guess I did.

MILDRED. Oh, all right, then. After I sing "Ah, Sweet Mystery," and make sure you don't start until I'm finished with that last note. It's the best part of the song. Go on, Ruthann.

RUTHANN. You're a beautiful bride, Naomi.

MILDRED. Go Ruthann! Stop gabbin'!

(*RUTHANN starts down the aisle as NAOMI pops up through the Porta Potty transom and takes a picture. FAYE pauses then follows Ruthann down the aisle; NAOMI again jumps up to the transom and takes a picture. As FAYE progresses down the aisle the Hawaiian MUSIC possesses her and she becomes a little bit too seductive in her walk. VIOLET struggles to get up but can't quite make it.*)

MILDRED. (*Noticing Violet.*) C'mon, Violet, you're holdin' up the ceremony.
VIOLET. I'm tryin', Mildred, but I can't seem to get up.
MILDRED. Well, c'mon. People are waitin'.

(VIOLET struggles a little while longer then proceeds down the aisle by "walking" her chair, with her still in it. NAOMI jumps up for another picture. MILDRED pauses for a moment then begins her walk and once again, NAOMI jumps up to take another picture.
Now the big moment has arrived. The DOOR to the Porta Potty flies open and there's NAOMI. SHE's carrying a huge bouquet of plastic daisies and has her Instamatic camera slung around her neck. SHE begins her walk and as she does SHE takes pictures of everyone. The FLASHES cause the wedding party to stumble.)

MILDRED. For the love of ... put that thing away, Naomi. I swear you're just lethal with that thing.

(Eternally the bride, NAOMI proceeds on.and we notice that the toilet paper from the Porta Potty has gotten cuaght in her veil. And as NAOMI heads toward the altar, the toilet paper follows.)

MILDRED. (*Referring to the toilet paper.*) Naomi, you plannin' to take that all the way to Nashville with you?
BUBBA. (*Flipping through his Parson's manual.*) We're gathered here today to join Naomi Louise Farkle and Luther Sylvester Carson, in holy matrimony. If there is anyone here who knows of any reason why these two should not be joined

in this divine union, let him speak now, or forever hold his peace.
VIOLET. Oh.

(EVERYONE looks at Violet.)

VIOLET. *(Sheepishly.)* Sorry ...
BUBBA. I believe at this time Miss Naomi Louise Farkle and Mr. Luther Sylvester Carson would like to read their own vows that they have written for each other. Miss Farkle?
NAOMI. Thank you, Parson Bedford. *(NAOMI reaches under her veil taking out a small sheet of paper which she noisily unfolds.)* This is entitled: "To My Lovey Husband To Be."
FAYE. I helped her on this, y'know.
MILDRED. Good heavens ...
NAOMI. *(As NAOMI reads FAYE mouths the words.)*
"Honey, I love you with all my heart and soul.
And how much I love you, you'll never know.
If somebody had told me years ago,
That someday you'd be my baby,
I would've told them that they were crazy!

But here you are and here am I,
And may our love fly high, high, high!

I really adore you, my little lovey,
And I'm just so excited that you're gonna be my hubby."
FAYE. *(Crying.)* That's so beautiful.

(NAOMI turns to take a picture of FAYE who instantly stops crying, smiles, then cries again.)

BUBBA. Oh, and now for Mr. Luther Sylvester Carson.

LUTHER. My turn? Oh. (*HE nervously unfolds a small sheet of paper.*) Ahem ... I ... uh ... don't have a title for this one ... I'm sorry.

NAOMI. That's all right, honey bear. (*NAOMI takes a picture.*)

LUTHER. I'll just read ... ahem ... "Dear Naomi. I am very glad that you said yes to my proposal of marriage. You have made me very happy. Thank you. Your friend, Luther Carson. (*Pause while LUTHER looks around embarrassed.*)

NAOMI. (*Crying.*) Isn't that just about the sweetest thing you ever did hear?

BUBBA. And now, do you, Miss Naomi Louise Farkle, take ...

MILDRED. (*Interrupting.*) Oh, wait. I've gotta sing "Ah, Sweet Mystery." Bubba? Would you put in that other tape, please?

(*BUBBA turns to the tape player and inserts the second tape. On the tape we hear a piano tuning, a note which MILDRED tires to match, but can't quite do it. The piece begins and MILDRED becomes progressively more off-key until NAOMI can't stand it any longer and crosses and hits the stop button.*)

LUTHER. (*Sarcastically.*) Well, *that* was pretty.

MILDRED. Shut up, Luther ...

BUBBA. And now do you, Miss Naomi Louise Farkle ...

RUTHANN. Wait, not yet. Faye has this poem she's gonna read. Go ahead, Faye.

FAYE. Well … I … uh … need to stand in front. (*FAYE pushes Naomi away.*) Can you scoot over some, Naomi?

(*NAOMI stumbles back.*)

FAYE. Thanks. Naomi and Luther … I wrote this very special poem for you last night after hours of gruelin' creative deliberation. It is entitled "Weddin' Bells." (*Pause as FAYE clears her throat.*)
Ding, dong, ding, dong.
Ging, gong, ging, gong.
    MILDRED. (*Aside.*) Sounds Chinese …
    FAYE.
Ring the happy, joyous, weddin' bells
Throughout the countryside.

Peasants, poor and tired, dance in
Jubilation in the village square,
As donkeys, chickens, goats, and other
Farmyard inhabitants,
Raise their voices like a chorus of
Angels.
    VIOLET. (*Weakly.*) Oh, y'all … I feel kinda funny.
    MILDRED. (*To Violet.*) Sssshhhhh …
    FAYE.
Flowers, like drunken sailors,
Dance wildly in the wind.
And the bride, like the flowers,
Dances for joy with her newly
Betrothed husband,
As the wind whips around her dress.
    VIOLET. (*Louder.*) OH!

FAYE.
And she smiles.
S-M-I-L-E-S.
Smiles.
    VIOLET. OHHHHHHH!

(EVERYONE stops and stares at Violet.)

    VIOLET. Y'all ... I'm not sure, but I think I'm about to
have a baby.

(ALL are quiet for a second, then pandemonium.)

    NAOMI. Good gravy boat Marie, what are we gonna do?
    FAYE. Put your head between your legs, Violet.
    DELBERT. *(To Bubba.)* Parson Bedford, I think you'd
better hurry up the ceremony just a bit.
    BUBBA. *(Quickly.)* And now, do you Miss Naomi Louise
Farkle, take Mr. Luther Sylvester Carson, to be your lawfully
wedded husband?
    NAOMI. Now, Violet, sugar ... don't you worry about a
thing. Why we'll have you at that ole hospital in nothin' flat.
    VIOLET. Ohhhhh!!! Hurry ...
    MILDRED. Naomi? Bubba just asked you if you'd marry
Luther. My stars, pay attention at your own weddin'.
    NAOMI. What? Oh ... I do ... I do. Here Violet, let me get
a picture of the baby.

*(NAOMI sets the camera as FAYE, RUTHANN and
    MILDRED "tableau" around her.)*

VIOLET.   (*As NAOMI is taking the picture.*) *OHHHHHH!!!*

NAOMI. Oh, that's a good one.

MILDRED. Delbert, here are my car keys. You go pull my car around. (*Hands keys to DELBERT.*)

DELBERT. All right, Mildred. I'll be back in a flash. (*HE exits.*)

FAYE. Violet, do you think you can walk?

VIOLET. Noooooooohhhhhhhhh!!!

MILDRED. Here, we'll have to carry her out in her chair, then. Luther you get on one side and Bubba, you get on the other.

(*BUBBA and LUTHER move into place.*)

BUBBA. And do you, Mr. Luther Sylvester Carson take Miss Naomi Louise Farkle to be your lawfully wedded wife?

LUTHER. I do!

BUBBA. By the power invested in me by Poplar Mechanics Magazine, I now pronounce you man and wife. (*BUBBA hands Violet his manual, which SHE holds open for him to read from as THEY lift her up.*) You may kiss the bride.

(*LUTHER and NAOMI kiss.*)

NAOMI. Oh, the bouquet. I gotta throw the weddin' bouquet!

MILDRED. Oh, for land's sake, Naomi. Faye's the only single girl here. Why don't you just save yourself the time and trouble and just hand it to her?

(As LUTHER and BUBBA followed by NAOMI are carrying VIOLET:)

NAOMI. Here we go ... one, two, three ... *(NAOMI pitches the bouquet over Violet and FAYE catches it.)*

FAYE. Did you see that, Mildred? I caught it! I caught the bouquet! That means I'm next to get married!

MILDRED. Congratulations, honey.

DELBERT. *(Rushes back in.)* O.k. ... the car's here. Let's go.

FAYE. Did you see me catch it, Delbert? Maybe fate's tryin' to tell us something. Maybe this is Kismet?

DELBERT. *(Indicating bouquet.)* No, Faye ... I think those are daffodils.

FAYE. Huh?

BUBBA. *(Still reading from his Parson's manual.)* Marriage is a sacred institution ...

(ALL exit with ad libs of "Shut up, Bubba," "Oh ... I'm so excited," "Good gravy boat, Marie," and VIOLET screaming at the top of her lungs.)

End of Play

THE FAITH COUNTY THEME SONG

1. It's a back-water burg,
A one-horse town,
As boring as can be.
Out here somewhere in the middle of nowhere,
Smack dab in Faith County.

You can have your hair done,
Or your Beehive spun,
At the beautiful Bee-Luv-Lee.
Or go down to the diner where you'll never find a finer,
Cup of Violet Farkle's coffee.

Well, Mildred, Harry, Bubba and Lucy, Luther, Delbert,
And Ruthann and Naomi,
With Lottie and Gladys, Bud, Violet and Faye all live,
In Faith County.

2. Mineola is a place where everyone knows your face,
So it's very simple to see.
There's nothing to do and everyone is dull,
Who lives in Faith County.

So pull up a chair and let down your hair,
Get ready to slap your knee.
'Cause we're gonna have a ball with usin's and y'all,
And the folks in Faith County.

Ch: Faith County, the county place to be!
Faith County, it's home sweet home to me!

www.ingramcontent.com/pod-product-compliance
Lightning Source LLC
Chambersburg PA
CBHW070649120726
47909CB00004B/1645